THE HONEY PACK CHRONICLES

A. MONIQUE

Copyright © 2023 by A. Monique

All rights reserved.

No part of this book may be reproduced in any form or by any electronic or mechanical means, including information storage and retrieval systems, without written permission from the author, except for the use of brief quotations in a book review.

The Honey Pack Chronicles

Author A. Monique

ABOUT THE AUTHOR

A. Monique was born and raised in East Chicago, IN. She still currently resides in Indiana with her family. A. Monique discovered her love for books and good stories in all different genres at the age of thirteen, with a special interest in Urban Fiction; even writing some of her own short stories and poems. It wasn't until after beta reading and the encouragement of friends and family, that she discovered her own talent.

Connect and Follow Me!

https://www.amazon.com/author/a.monique

Prettyreads.com

IG and Tik Tok: Author_A_Monique

Join my Facebook group: Pretty Readers or Angela Johnson

Everything that glitters ain't gold.

When you're dealing with a *honey pack* you'd better proceed with caution.

One can never know what the outcome will be…

CHAPTER 1

*D*own in the DM
      Syxx

The fact that I'm young, fly, and flashy but, yet home alone with no motion on a Saturday night was beyond me. I lost all my hoes because they called themselves having morals and shit. Now everybody wants to be in a relationship! Fuck that! I ain't wifing none of these tramps! I'm thirty-three years old, no kids, and I still have way too much living to do to be settled down with one person. I had one favorite girl, Vysion, that I kicked it hard with for the last three years, but she started getting too clingy and wanting to do couple shit like holding hands in public and going out on dates. I had to tell her ass that we don't do that type of stuff over here. To make matters worse she kept wanting to take pictures and post me all over The Great Future Hendrix's internet and that was just fucking insane! She got mad and now called herself cutting me off. The fucking audacity of these chicks! She'll be back though. These broads love to label me as toxic but they always came back. Who's really the toxic one, me or them?

Now I'm forced to sit here and scroll on social media, sip on this *Don Julio Anejo* and hit my blunt until I pass out for the night, I suppose. I decided to hit my boy P up and see what the moves were.

He's been my dawg ever since we had to go upside some nigga's heads in middle school for roasting him about his government name, which is Preston. He hates that name. I exited from my timeline and sent him a text.

Me: Aye nigga what you on?

P: Shit, chillin my boy. You?

Me: You trying to hit some spots tonight and find some bitches to slide in?

P: Man, it is a lot of parties going on tonight, but I'm about to slide into something warm. I already had this play set up. You feel me? I think she got a few cousins and sisters. If you want me to, I can ask her to put you on, my boy.

Me: Aw yeah, I feel you, but naw koo I'm good. Have you a good night my nig.

P: Oh, I will. I'm about to grab me and shorty one of those honey packs so it's lit!

Me: That's what's up nigga, be smooth.

I sat my phone down, confusion etched across my face, because what the hell is a honey pack and why is this nigga so excited about it? My nigga P was always into some freaky shit with women. Shit that I could never see myself doing. He talks about eating these bitch's asses like it's his favorite snack and pastime sport, Yuck! So shit, maybe I don't even want to know what a damn honey pack is, if that nigga is hyped up about it.

However, my curiosity was getting the best of me right now, so I felt inclined to at least investigate it.

I went on my search engine to try and Google that shit because I needed to know what I was missing out on.

To my surprise, there were multiple reviews and videos with people raving about the *honey pack,"* and how it put them on demon time. One man even wrote, *"Man, that damn honey pack had my dick rock hard for a whole night! I love this shit!"* That was all I needed to see! It's a must that I find me a pretty, thick lil' thang to try this super honey that keep niggas on brick hard out on. I might even hit Vysion up because I know if Daddy calls, she's coming. She was mad at me right now, but this dick would make it right. I could just tell her that I'm sorry and that I'd consider an exclusive relationship. She'd be putty in my hands. Just as I was about to scroll down my phone's contact list to see who I could potentially hit up, before settling on Vys and her never-ending emotions; I heard a ding on my phone which alerted me that there was someone direct messaging me. Perplexed as to who could be hitting me up this late, and it not being about some money, I opened my *Messenger* and noticed that I had a request from a female. I always screened my messages to see what motherfuckas be wanting before I actually accept the request that alerts them that I've seen their messages. This shit was right on time, so I opened the actual message, and it was from a woman by the name of Gryffyn Davis. I read on curiously.

Gryffyn: Hey Sexy! I was scrolling on here and came across your profile on *People You May Know*. I liked what I saw so now I'm hitting you up to see if maybe you'd be willing to meet up with me for drinks tonight?

"Damn, this shorty ain't playing! She's really trying to fuck with a playa," I spoke out loud to myself. Before I could get too excited, I had to go on her page and do a little background check. I needed to go on there and see what those angles were looking like. To my surprise, this chick was fucking bad! I couldn't really tell how tall she was, but her full body shots and selfies had my dick standing at attention, ready to blow! I loved me a thick and chocolate woman. It just did something to my soul! Then she had the nerve to have some thick and full lips too. I couldn't keep her fine ass waiting any longer, I had to respond fast. But I didn't want to come off as a thirsty ass nigga. After all, I was Syxx Tha Fucking OG!

SyxxThaOG: What's up Ms. Lady? I appreciate you hitting ya boy up. I like what I see as well, what do you have in mind?

Gryffyn: Hmm, well there is a chill little spot on State Street called The Bureau Bar, do you want to meet me there? I can be there within the hour, if that's cool with you? My treat.

SyxxThaOG: Aw yeah shorty, that's cool. I'll check you out in a minute, aight?

Gryffyn: Okay boo, I'll see you then!

I logged out of my social media, sitting stuck for a minute. This shit was crazy! The bitch is fine as hell, thick as hell and she's willing to treat a nigga out the first time? Aw yeah, I'm going to have to put this dick so far up in her that when she burps, she's burping up my kids! I snapped out of my daze and looked at the time on my watch.

"10:05 pm, shit!" Let me jump my ass in the shower really quick so I can go meet my new potential victim for the night.

I wanted to have this bitch so ready to bust it open that I made sure to put that shit on! I was stepping out fresh as hell! Damn near anything I put on my chocolate, six-foot, three-inch frame looked good though. I did a quick line up on my face as well. My thick and full beard drove the ladies crazy every time, and I had recently gotten my locs re-twisted, so I was good to go. I made sure to spray on a little of my Ombre Leather cologne by Tom Ford, which made panties fall off. I grabbed my Woods off the table and was out the door by 10:45 pm.

I knew exactly where *The Bureau Bar* was and knew that it wouldn't take me but about fifteen minutes to get there, so I was making good timing. Women got irritated when men were late, so I didn't want to have that fine ass girl waiting on me. I didn't want to chance her not giving up the goods, so my black ass was going to be on time. I cranked my radio up listening to my fearless leader, Future and I pulled off. I drove a block up and was stopped by a red light, so I decided to light my blunt up for the ride. As I inhaled on one the purest strains of green out here, I glanced to my right and saw a gas station on the corner. I instantly thought back to the online reviews about honey packs that said they could be purchased at any gas station. As I was coming out of my daze, was the light changed to green, so I pulled off. I had a nagging urge to look for this so-called *super honey*, so I made a sharp turn into the gas station's parking lot. Before I could change my mind, I smashed the blunt in the ashtray and hopped out of my brand-new BMW truck. I said that I was a lonely nigga, not a broke one, keep up!

I walked inside and approached the window in search of a small packet labeled, *The Honey Pack*. The owner of the gas station was looking at me as if I was a crazy person because I was just standing there looking around.

"Hey Syxx, my brudder, what can I get for you? You want usual, buddy?"

I laughed at Ahmed because he always tried to be cool. I was a regular there and usually I would just grab something to drink and a pack of Backwoods, but today was different.

"Uh, naw Ahmed, I want one of those, um, *honey packs*."

"Oh, you want honey my friend, okay, I know what you want do to da ladies, huh?" Ahmed winked.

"Man bro, just give me the shit. I'm about to be late fucking with you, and why are you winking at me, G?"

"Oh, Syxx, sorry, sorry. I wink because you whisper, brudder." Ahmed said in his thick accent while handing me the foil packet.

That's when I realized that I was indeed whispering. I chuckled at the revelation and paid Ahmed.

"Good looking out, bro."

"Enjoy Syxx, my friend."

I did a light jog back to my car and got in quickly. Once I was inside, I looked around checking my surroundings because I had to keep my head on a swivel in these streets. The enemy was always lurking, and they were always closer than you'd think. I hit the push to start button on my car and peeled off into the night. I had some pussy to get to.

CHAPTER 2

I pulled up to my destination in 10 minutes flat. From the outside, I could tell that there was a nice little crowd in there. I found a decent parking spot, gave myself a once over in the mirror and hopped out. I walked inside feeling myself. The *Don Julio* that I'd already consumed, coupled with the weed and now the bass from the music playing, made me feel like I was *That Nigga* coming through! I looked around and saw my date for the night sticking out like a sore thumb sitting at the bar. She must've noticed me as well, because we made eye contact, and she waved me over. Making my way across the crowded room, I made sure to put an extra smooth ass bop in my walk. Shorty was all smiles as I approached her and shit, I can't lie, so was I. This girl was so damn fine, I almost caught myself stammering over my words when I spoke to her.

"H-h-hey Gorgeous, what's up with you?" I cleared my throat and stuck my hand out for a handshake.

"Unt Uh, I'm a hugger, so come here, cutie. I'm good, how are you?"

Her voice was as soft and smooth as silk coming out of those juicy ass lips, and this woman had the nerve to smell like vanilla and berries or some shit like that! Sweet and fruity.

"I'm cool, mama."

"Good, now have a seat and tell me about yourself. But, before you do, what are you drinking tonight?"

"Uh, I'll take a double shot of Tequila Anejo by *Don Julio* straight up."

"Okay, I see you," Gryffyn chuckled.

I watched this fine specimen flag down the bartender and place our drink orders in awe. "And keep them coming," I heard her say. It's something about watching a woman take charge like that that turned me on. Now I was determined to break her down in the bedroom.

We made small talk until the bartender placed our drinks down in front of us. I immediately picked mine up and took a swig. I don't know why this woman has me feeling nervous like I'm feminine or some shit!

"So why did you really hit me up, man? Bit- I mean women don't usually hop in DM's trying to link up. What you on with me?"

"Well, I don't know what kind of women you're used to but I'm the type that if I see something I like, I go for it. I also always get what I want." Gryffyn winked.

"Oh, is that right? Well, I always get what I want as well so maybe we'll both win tonight."

"Yeah, maybe."

I watched Gryffyn sip the contents of her glass through the straw and all I could think about is what her succulent lips would do to my dick later.

"Syxx, are you listening to me?"

"Yeah, baby. Why, what's up?"

"I'm talking to you, and you seem to be in a daze, are you okay?"

Shit, I'm caught.

"Aw, yeah girl, I'm just mesmerized by how beautiful you are. Where did you say you were from again?"

"I didn't say but I'm originally from Houston. I recently moved out here to follow up on a few prospective acting jobs. I've been staying with a friend of mine."

"Oh okay, that's what's up. Do you want to get out of here? We've been sitting here chatting for a few hours and they're about to close in a little bit."

"Yeah, sure, are you ready to call it a night or do you want to kick it a little more," Gryffyn asked with seduction lacing her sweet voice.

"I'm sure we can find something to get into, just let me hit the restroom really quick, cool?"

"Go handle your business, babe."

I got up and headed in the direction of the men's restroom as quickly as possible. Everything that came out of Gryffyn's mouth sounded like a sweet love song. I had to keep myself in check or I would've been walking through this place with a stiff dick. I made it into an empty stall and took a leak. Once I was finished, I went to the sink, washed my hands and ended up staring at myself in the mirror. It was time to show this chick exactly who I am. It was then that I remembered that I had the honey in my pocket. I fished my pockets for it until I located the *honey pack*. It was now or never and since I'm not a simp ass nigga, I tore at the corner and braced myself. "Here's to my one ticket to pound town!" Just like that, I drank from the foil packet until it was empty. "Ugh, this shit is nasty as hell!" I complained.

Not really knowing what to expect, I threw the empty package away and rejoined my date at the bar.

"You ready to dip out of here, sexy?" I asked.

"Yeah Daddy, I was waiting for you," Gryffyn smiled sweetly as I helped her down from the barstool.

"Okay, so do you want to follow me back to my house or ride with me? I'll take you home when you're ready to leave, if that's cool?"

"I actually took a rideshare, so it looks like I'm riding with you." Gryffyn's smile reached her eyes.

"Yo, stop looking and smiling at me like that, girl," I told her as we walked to my car.

"Like what?" Gryffyn feigned innocence, clutching her imaginary pearls.

"Like you want me to fuck you right here in this parking lot."

Gryffyn walked into my personal space closing the gap between us, stood on her toes and whispered, "You can fuck me anywhere, baby. I don't run from or duck any action."

Fuuuuuccckkkkk! I don't know if it was the sexiness that this woman exuded or her lip brushing against my ear while she whispered that freaky ass shit to me, but the holy spirit in me activated and I was ready to take this woman down!

I wrapped my arm around her waist, pulling her into me, lifting her up with one arm, sitting her on the hood of my car and tongued her down. She wrapped her thick thighs around me and positioned her warm middle, right- center on my crotch. I slid my hand underneath the leather skirt she had been wearing, only to discover that she had no panties on. I sent a quick and silent thank you up to the big homey in the sky, because this woman was indeed freaky as hell.

"No panties tonight, huh?" I said inserting one and then two fingers inside of her now dripping slit.

"Nope," was Gryffyn's only reply as she bit her lip and gyrated her hips against my fingers.

That's when I started going crazy in her pussy. My fingers were doing sign language and throwing up gang signs in her shit.

"Ooh shit," Gryffyn moaned, "that's my spot right there."

Shit, say less. The more she moaned and rode my fingers the faster my pace picked up. Right when I felt Gryffyn's walls beginning to thump and tighten up on me...

Boom!

We both jumped, startled trying to figure out where the loud noise was coming from! I looked down and realized that my gun had fallen from the holster to the pavement.

"Shit! Are you okay?" I asked her but I was trying to get my own heart rate to slow down.

"Yes, I'm okay. That really scared me," she laughed and hopped down off the hood.

"Yeah, that shit shook me too. How about we go back to my crib?"

"Sounds like a plan."

Gryffyn walked around to the passenger side of the car and

stopped. Just as I was about to get in, I noticed her reluctance to do the same.

"What's wrong?" I asked perplexed.

"I'm waiting for you to open the car door for me," she said, matter of factly.

"Oh, my fault." I laughed but inside I was thinking that this bitch is different. No woman had ever required me to open a damn car door, or any door for that matter.

I didn't want to fuck up my play for the night, so I did what was expected of me and opened the door for her to get in, waited until she was comfortable and then closed the door afterwards. I walked back to the driver's side rolling my eyes. I really hoped that this girl's pussy was worth all this effort, because if not, I'm kicking her ass right out. Once I was behind the wheel, I went straight for my wood and lit that thang right up. Gryffyn sat silently watching me. I was slightly annoyed by her low-key demanding for me to open the door for her. I'm a hood ass nigga, I don't do all that cute shit! If I was on that type of time, I would be with Vysion. I took a long pull from my blunt and released that shit. Now, I was ready to continue with my night. I looked over to Gryffyn and I could've sworn she was smirking at me. I looked back over to her, and she was nodding her head to the music. Gotdamn, this girl is fine! *This weed got me tweaking.*

CHAPTER 3

We pulled up to my building and I didn't waste any time getting out of the car. I headed towards the front gate and noticed that Gryffyn was still inside the car. I walked over to her side and threw my hands in the air.

"What are you doing, man? Are you getting out?"

"Yeah, when you open the car door for me."

"Oh, my fucking God, come on, G!" I yelled, opening the door frustrated that this girl was doing the most.

Gryffyn got out and adjusted herself without saying a word.

We walked through the gate side by side. I went to my front door, unlocked it and pushed it open so that she could go through first.

As she walked by me, she looked me in my eyes, touched my chin and said, "lesson one is chivalry, love. You will display that whenever I'm in your presence."

Who is this bitch? Let me hurry up and fuck her so I can send her on her way! I thought to myself.

I didn't even get the whole thought out. By the time I locked the door and turned around to face my company, she was standing in the middle of the floor, butt naked with only the heels on that she wore that night. At this point I couldn't even remember how badly she had just annoyed me. My dick now had full control of my body! I had to keep it playa and regain my composure, so I smiled and slowly began taking my shirt off.

"Yeah? That's what you're on?"

Gryffyn didn't say a word, just used her finger to summons me closer to her, and that's exactly what I did. This woman's body was so cold and well put together that she would put any of your favorite female rapper's BBL to shame. When I finally made it over to her, she dropped down to her knees and pulled my dick out. Now, I knew that the honey must've began to run its course because it felt as though my dick had some type of extra sensitivity to it. Every five seconds this motherfucker was springing to action! Right now, was no different. I was ready to be balls deep inside of this girl!

I opened my eyes and looked down to discover this nasty freak bitch pulled out a honey packet of her own!

Gryffyn backed me up against the wall next to my bedroom door, ripped open the foil packet with her teeth and spread the thick contents all over my dick. She then squeezed the remainder all over her lips, which made my dick rock up even more to the point that it hurt. She stuck her tongue out and seductively licked the thick substance from her lips in a counter- clockwise motion. Gryffyn left just enough on her sexy ass lips so that it was still coated. She took my whole length down her throat and my knees almost gave out when I realized that this Godsend of a woman had a no-gag reflex!

When I felt my nut trying to rise to the surface, I had to snap back to reality and realize what the fuck was going on! I took a step back from Gryffyn, releasing my throbbing dick from her mouth that felt vacuum sealed.

"Damn girl, who are you?" I asked out of breath.

"Shut the fuck up!"

On that note I clutched my imaginary pearls, as females did, appalled. Gryffyn stood up and walked back towards me, once again closing the distance and threw her right leg; still wearing her heels; might I add, over my shoulder. My first reaction was to secure that thick motherfucker, so I did. She then proceeded to grab my dick and inserted it inside of herself. I almost gave in like a goofy as soon as I entered her euphoric hole and cum instantaneously, but I didn't! Gryffyn was literally riding me while standing straight up! I had to attempt to take control of the situation, so each time she drove her wet ass pussy into me, I gave her the strongest pumps I could muster up. There is no way I could let a female fuck me like some bitch ass nigga! I do the fucking around here, or so I thought.

"Ah!"

First pump, yeah there it goes, I thought.

Now, I'm drilling her.

Second pump.

"Oh shit," she moaned.

Yeah, I got her ass now!

Third pump, and damn this feels like some sort of witchery.

Just when I got into a groove and got her where I wanted her, she snatched her leg down, turned around and backed her ass into me. When my dick slid out of her, all that could be heard was a soft thud as my penis slapped my thigh. She had to have one of the wettest and tightest vaginas ever! I didn't waste any time this go round so I put my dick back in her myself. This pussy was feeling more and more like home, damnit!

Gryffyn started off grinding on my dick slowly. She was literally twerking on the D. The way she was gripping her ankles and rolling up and down on my dick had to be blasphemy! Her pussy on my dick had to be similar to the way butter melts on hot bread. All I need right now is a blunt.

I lost focus and my balance when Gryffyn stopped doing whatever voodoo she was doing to me. I tried to gather my composure, but this bitch had yet another trick in her bag.

"Secure my legs daddy, okay?" Gryffyn voiced.

"Ye-Yeah, I got you."

Shit, I really wanted to yell out "Anything for you, Queen!" Instead, I put my focus on Gryffyn.

I was now watching this woman position herself into an upside-down position, but I didn't have to wonder anymore as to what was happening though. This woman was now head down in a handstand, while I had both of her legs interlocked in my arms. *Gotdamn is this what honey does?*

Once Gryffyn was secured in her position, she then looked back at me, winked and blew me a kiss.

"Eat."

"What you say?" I heard the bitch loud and clear, but I wanted to be sure she said what I think she did.

"Eat this motherfucker," she demanded without even looking up at me.

No cap, my first mind is telling me to drop this girl on the floor and put her ass out of my spot, but I want this pussy bad. I'm not a pussy licker, that's just not my modus operandi, I don't even know the first thing about it. I slay the cat so good that women never even think to ask me for head, and I've never fucked with someone that I wanted to perform the act with. Not even Vysion. *I wonder what Future would do in this situation.* I pushed all my thoughts to the side and thought about how good the vagina before me was so far, and how I wanted to see what else was in store for the night. *Fuck it,* I thought as I saw Gryffyn look up towards the kitchen.

"Alexa, start a Trey Songz playlist." Gryffyn commanded my device that was on the kitchen counter.

The first song that came on was "Dive In" and I was pissed! My Alexa is now an opp ass bitch.

I reluctantly put my face in Gryffyn's middle and found her clit. One thing I know is a woman's body. I may not be a head giver, but I'll play in some pussy all night. Once my tongue found Gryffyn's button I began to lick and suck on it like it was the last meal I'd ever consume. I went nose deep in her pussy, not leaving any leftovers. Watching her squirm while still balancing herself was a turn on like no other. Seeing that only made me want to go harder to see if she would get weak and let go.

"Aah, yes! Get it, baby!" Gryffyn moaned out.

That shit was music to my ears! I was either doing a good job or she was a good ass actress! Nonetheless, Gryffyn hyping me up made my head big a little.

Eating pussy isn't that bad, I thought.

"Ooh, right there Syxx!"

I started really feeling myself and began fucking her tight hole with my tongue which drove her crazy!

"Ohmigod!" Gryffyn yelled while thrusting her hips into my mouth harder.

Damn this girl is strong.

"Yeah, give it here, baby," I encouraged.

Gryffyn did just that, she gave it all to me alright. For the first time I allowed a woman to squirt her juices in my mouth. I licked all that shit up too. It's just something about this girl that's making me want to step outside of my sexual box.

"Put it in, baby," she purred seductively.

That is exactly what the fuck I did! I put my hard and pussy juice-soaked penis inside of the demon before me and went to work. If we weren't butt ass naked someone walking in on us would've assumed that Gryffyn was just twerking on me, until they caught a glimpse of me looking crazy from how good this girl's pussy was feeling. She is so damn talented! Not only that, but I haven't come across a woman yet that can take my dick whole the way that Gryffyn was doing. Most chicks tire out easily or just simply can't take all of what I'm giving.

"Damn, baby, slow down before you make me cum."

"Hell naw, daddy, that's the whole point, to cum. Now give me that nut so I can get it back up and suck the next one out of you."

The way those words fell from her lips seemed to cause my dick to rock up and the nut that had been building up began oozing from my tip like an erupting volcano.

"Aargh, fuck!" I yelled out.

"Yes, daddy! Give it all here!"

Gryffyn kept her hips rotating in a circular motion, but my legs began to weaken. Gryffyn refused to slow her pace down causing me to let every seed I had in me out inside of her walls.

"Wait, wait, wait! Hold up!" My voice was hoarse at this point."

I had just come hard as hell and Gryffyn kept going.

"Mmm Mmm, there is nothing to wait for. I'm just getting started."

Gotdammit man, I hope I didn't just get her pregnant but if I did, I ain't mad at it. No hot girl summer for you boo. You'll have to sit that good ol' nine months and six weeks out, I joked to myself. I had never wanted to trap a woman before, but there is a first time for everything. I'll get this girl pregnant just to ensure that I'd get to hit that again.

CHAPTER 4

Snapping me out of my reverie was Gryffyn leading me across the way to my own bedroom as if she had been here before. After the fat ass nut, she had just pulled out of me, she was now in charge. I'm just following her lead at this point in the game. Gryffyn walked me over to my King-sized bed and pushed me down on my back. She then straddled me and hovered her pussy over my pelvic area. The warmth radiating from her vagina was turning me on. I wanted to plunge right back into her, but my dick wasn't going. That last orgasm put me down, I needed a minute to recover, or so I thought. Gryffyn stared seductively in my eyes, tugging at her bottom lip with her teeth and began to rock slowly, backwards and forward. She was still hovering and barely making contact with my penis, but her actions had my body slightly convulsing with every movement she made. I can't lie, I was about to cum all over myself and my dick hadn't even gotten back hard yet. To distract myself from the embarrassment that was sure to come next, I reached up, grabbed her breasts and slowly started massaging them.

"Mmmmm," Gryffyn moaned.

"You like that?"

"Yes baby, do it harder."

I did what Gryffyn requested and kneaded her breasts and nipples in between my fingers, eventually putting each one in my mouth. Gryffyn had the perfect set of titties, more than a hand and mouthful, just the way I prefer.

"Oh, so he's being stubborn I see," Gryffyn asked looking down at my limp member.

"Naw, Bae, you just took a lot out of me, and I need a few minutes, that's all." I replied nervously and partially embarrassed that my lil man's is acting up in front of company.

"We'll see about that."

Before I could process what she said, Gryffyn was flipping me on my stomach like I was a lil bitch! I was trying to understand what was happening. I also wanted to know how often this bitch goes to the gym because she's strong as hell!

Gryffyn reached under, flipped me over, and lifted me on all fours.

"Girl, what the fuck are you doing?" Gryffyn ignored me.

I'm a fucking gangsta, we don't...."

That was all I was able to get out before Gryffyn palmed my balls and swallowed my dick whole, again. I didn't have any more argument left once my dick was stuffed so far down her throat, I could've sworn I was touching the bottom of her stomach. The back of her throat was feeling way too good. Gryffyn was sucking and licking on my shit like I had the best dick in the world. She began to do this humming thing, while massaging my balls and it had me ready to let off another round right down her esophagus. It's something about hearing the slurps from a woman's mouth as she's topping you off that'll have you ready to blow! The head was feeling way too good.

Gryffyn hummed some more and then that's when I almost lost it! I felt this bitch's nose tickling me and I panicked! Granted, she wasn't necessarily touching my ass, but it was way too close for fucking comfort!

"Aye man, get the fuck from off of me!" I jumped up quick as hell and ran to the other side of the room away from her. I looked down and realized that I'd grabbed one of the pillows off the bed, partially covering myself up.

It's fucking me up, because whatever she was doing actually felt good, but it felt like some other shit too. I won't even allow myself to think about.

"Baby, what's wrong, am I not making you feel good?"

Gryffyn looked concerned but I thought I saw a hint of humor in her facial expression, and it was damn near throwing me off.

"Yeah man, but I don't like that shit, so don't do it no more. Stay the fuck away from my ass region."

"Yes, daddy, now come over here and fuck me some more." Gryffyn laid back in the bed and spread her legs wide open, motioning with her index finger for me to come to her.

As badly as I wanted the night to be over now, I couldn't just walk the other way. I had to see this shit all the way through. I looked down and my dick was back in the game and ready to go. I slowly and cautiously climbed into the bed with Gryffyn, and she was smiling at me.

Damn this bitch is beautiful. Maybe that's why I'm even allowing her in my presence. I just hope I don't end up regretting this shit.

"What's wrong, Syxx? What are you waiting for? This pussy isn't going to fuck itself," Gryffyn purred.

"You know what? Turn your ass around, it's time for Daddy to take control."

"Ooh, okay then."

Gryffyn did exactly as was instructed and put that ass in the air for me. I gave that big, juicy motherfucking bubble the strongest smack that I could muster up.

"Oh shit!"

"Yeah, oh shit, now shut the fuck up and take this dick!"

I positioned Gryffyn just how I wanted her and plunged my dick right into her wet slit with no warning.

"Goddamn, what are you doing to me? This shit is way too tight, who are you? Satan"

"Yes," was Gryffyn's only reply as she moaned out different expletives.

I had to give this woman everything I have because I have never been inside a better pussy! This thang is top tier and the reason why she acts the way she does is because she knows it too. There is no way that a woman should be allowed to walk around with this kind of weapon in her pants. I don't know why she's single but I'm definitely going to change that.

"Tell me how this dick feels, Gryffyn."

"Oooh, it feels so good, daddy."

The sound of her voice makes my dick harder, so I gotta keep her talking to me.

"You gon be mine, you know that?"

"Mmm, yes, baby, I'm yours."

Gryffyn started throwing that ass back harder, so I wrapped my hand around her throat and began to thrust harder, stronger.

Gryffyn took it each time and even began sucking on my index finger.

Aww hell naw, I gotta do something so that I don't bust yet.

I had to do something and quick because the nut that wanted to escape me was massive! I snatched my dick out of Gryffyn and buried my face right in her ass.

It was at this very second, I knew that my player card was about to go out the window. Future would be so disappointed in me.

I didn't care anymore at this point, so I ate. I ate the groceries like I was an inmate on Death Row and Gryffyn's ass was my last requested meal. I ate it like someone offered me 100 million dollars and dared me to eat it. I ate this motherfucker like it was reparations.

I could tell Gryffyn was shocked too but she surely didn't try and stop a nigga. In fact, this damn girl put a deeper arch in her back granting me full access.

"Aah, yes Syxx, right there!"

Gryffyn was so into what I was doing that she reached behind me and held my head in place. I figured she was about to come so I shook my face side to side in it and inserted one and then two fingers inside of her dripping pussy. I don't know if it's still the honey, liquor or the fact that I'm really enjoying the sex with this woman that's getting me out of character, but this shit is wild!

I talk so much shit to P about eating ass and giving head and I'm over here doing the shit like I'm a veteran or something like that.

I felt Gryffyn's body begin to tense up and she started shaking so I knew it was time.

"Omigod, Syxx! Don't fucking stop!"

Gryffyn was smashing all of that ass right on up against my face, damn near clapping my ears together and I kept licking.

Aah, Aah, Yesssssssss!"

She was now officially smothering me with that ass.

Once she was finished, she collapsed on the bed. That was my queue to fall back inside of that pussy so I could get my big one off and that's exactly what I did too.

"Naw, babygirl, ain't no breaks, remember? Didn't you tell me that?"

"Shut up Syxx," Gryffyn laughed.

I shut up alright. I grabbed her legs and pulled her into me. I leaned in and gave Gryffyn a kiss. (Another player rule broken) Gryffyn was receptive of my kiss though, and used her tongue to part my lips, gently inserting her tongue into my mouth. I can't even remember the last time I French kissed any chick; it was probably high school, but I was allowing it to happen with Gryffyn. I felt comfortable enough to do so. No cap, if Vysion ever found out, she'd probably kill me. For years, she's tried to do all that lovey dovey shit with me and I would dead that shit as soon as she attempted it, telling her that I wasn't into shit like that. Now, here I am doing the most with a bitch I just met.

I kissed Gryffyn for at least five whole minutes. We just kissed and rubbed on each other, and I fucked with every minute of it. I eventually broke the kiss and took each of Gryffyn's chocolate gumdrops into my mouth. I licked them and played with them until they both stood tall. I couldn't stop there, though, so I kissed all over the perfect canvas in front of me. I made sure to be slow and intentional with each kiss. Gryffyn watched me. Her face told me that she was ready to be fucked and I was ready to deliver.

I sat up on my knees hovering over a waiting Gryffyn and gave her one last kiss on the lips. That kiss was her only warning, because immediately after, I pushed her knees to her ears and dove deep! It was my turn to really show up and show out! I went in on Gryffyn's tight little pussy! My strokes were long and hit the back of her pussy with impact!

"What the fuck Syxx! Damn, baby!"

Gryffyn was losing her shit and I loved every moment of it!

"Oh, fuck daddy, you're fucking me so good!"

Yeah, I know.

I had Gryffyn pent up, legs over her head, giving her some long overdue hard dick!

Her ass folded after a while, cumming multiple times and calling out to God to save her at least a dozen times. Once she came the last time, I was finally ready for my big one. I picked up my pace, placing both of Gryffyn's perfectly toned legs on my shoulders, not missing a beat. I turned slightly to the left, making sure to hit every wall Gryffyn had, and I pounded her ass out until she eventually came again, and I busted one big, fat ass nut all inside of her throbbing walls.

It was my turn to collapse. I laid down next to a depleted and out of breath Gryffyn. No words had been spoken between us and within seconds we both passed out.

CHAPTER 5

I jumped up out of my sleep not knowing where I was and who I was with, I glanced around and remembered that I was in the comfort of my own home, so I relaxed a little. I looked up at the clock on my wall and saw that it was three pm. I threw my blankets back and sat up trying to piece my night together and it finally hit me that I brought company home. I looked over to the other side of the bed and it was empty. Slightly confused, I got up still naked with my dick sticking to my leg and walked into the master bathroom, inside of my bedroom. It was empty, so I relieved my full bladder and washed my hands. On my way out, I remembered that I was a regular ol' pussy and ass eater last night, so I brushed my teeth and gargled much longer than usual, fully disgusted at myself.

"I ain't fucking with that honey shit no more," I gave myself one last glance in the mirror, shook my head and proceeded to find last night's conquest.

Walking in and out of each room, I couldn't locate Gryffyn anywhere.

"Fuck it." Shrugging my shoulders, I proceeded into the kitchen.

I can't believe this bitch cut out on me after giving me that damn unicorn fairy pussy. Looking through my refrigerator further pissed me off because I'm hungry as fuck and that damn sex I had last night left a nigga starving.

"It ain't shit in this damn house to eat, man!"

My head whipped hard to the left.

"Wait, hold the fuck up, what's that smell?"

For some odd reason, the aroma of food hit my nostrils hard.

"I must be tweaking."

I followed the glorious scent, anyway, sniffing the air, as if I was a blood hound on to something. It led me all the way to my microwave. The shit is strange because I don't remember leaving anything in there. I'd been eating out at restaurants ever since me and Vysion started beefing. She was the cook around here. I can make little shit, but Vys kept a nigga's belly full of those fire ass home cooked meals she prepares.

I reached for the handle, pulling it open and in it were three warm containers of food inside.

"What the hell is this," I whispered to myself, looking around again to make sure Gryffyn wasn't about to pop out at me. I don't like being surprised and I would hate to have to knock her strong, pretty ass out for playing like that.

"Ayo, Gryffyn, you still here?" I called out once more.

She had to have placed the order, gotten the food and then left, but what kind of sense does that make?

Nevertheless, I pulled the food containers out and noticed they had come from Batter and Berries by looking at the restaurant's to-go order receipt. The shit smelled so good that for a brief moment I had forgotten all about Gryffyn and stabbed into the plate in front of me with my fork.

Shorty had done me a solid by ordering me The Super French Toast Flight; a spinach omelet and turkey sausage. The damn girl must be a psychic too, because French toast is a favorite of mine.

I dug right into the French toast first. I was so engulfed in the spread that I wasn't paying attention to my phone ringing non- stop. It was on vibration mode, so I didn't hear it. I reached over onto the other side of the kitchen island and saw that I had over forty missed calls and text messages combined.

I went through the calls that were sure to lace my pockets first, and then looked through the miscellaneous ones after. I had a few return calls from some of the women I attempted to link up with last night, but fuck them now, it's a new day.

I kept scrolling and saw that I had a few missed calls from Vysion.

"What the fuck does she want now?"

No cap, I really do be missing Vysion sometimes because she knows how to take care of a nigga, but she be wanting too much from me. I made a mental note to get back to her later. My thoughts were drifting off to my future baby mama, Miss Gryffyn.

I wonder if her fine, freaky ass is willing to cater to a real nigga like me and give me that King treatment.

I had a half of mind to hit her up and tell her to bring her ass back. Daddy hadn't dismissed her yet.

"Oh shit, I didn't even get her number!"

How did I let that happen? "Fuck!"

Remembering that Gryffyn was in my DM's, I decided to just reach out to her from there. Just as I opened the app to find the messages from last night, I noticed several notifications from my home security video app. I clicked on the alerts and saw the footage from mine and Gryffyn's trysts and smiled. I'd have to go back and revisit that one for sure. I went to the most recent one from outside the premises and pressed play.

The first slide was Gryffyn retrieving the food from the delivery driver. Once she entered the front door, I changed to the inside cameras. She put the food inside and placed it inside the microwave. Not long after, I saw her heading back towards the door to an awaiting car, which I'm assuming was a rideshare. As she walked out of the front door, she reached back inside to the glass table by the door and sat something on top, so I zoomed in to see that it was money.

"Why would she sit her money down?" I asked myself out loud.

I shook my head confusedly and continued watching, intently.

Gryffyn was finally outside the door, so I quickly switched the views of the camera back outside.

Before she walked off, she hit the bell to my Ring doorbell/camera. I exited the security app and went over to the Ring app, growing irritable at the login procedure. Once I was in, I hit the unmute button, thirsty to hear whatever she was saying and that's when Gryffyn's voice blared through the speaker.

"Hey Daddy."

I blushed.

"It was fun! I'll be in touch. Mwah!"

"Huh?" I blinked rapidly.

Gryffyn turned to walk off and then doubled back.

"Oh yeah, I left you a little something on the table. You were great! Maybe invest in a cleaning service, we kind of made a mess."

Gryffyn chuckled and lightly jogged to back of the car and just like that, she was gone.

"I know this bitch didn't! Who the fuck does she think she's playing with!" I seethed.

I quickly jumped up, knocking my phone to the floor and leaving the now cold food on the counter. I headed to my front room and just as Gryffyn said, she left some money on the table like I was a damn hoe being thanked! Picking the money up, I counted it and she left two-hundred dollars there. I threw that shit across the room, pissed off! In all of my years of fucking, no woman has ever treated me this way! The gall of this bitch to fuck me with that Houdini ass twat and leave me a gotdamn tip like I did her a service.

I marched my long-legged ass back into the kitchen and picked my phone up from the floor. I logged into my messenger app and tapped on Gryffyn's name:

SyxxThaOG: Aye man, what the fuck is up? Why would you leave like that and then put money on the table like I needed a hand-out or something?

I waited a minute to see if she would respond.

I looked up and realized that I had been sitting for ten minutes waiting, for nothing. No reply.

"Man, fuck this bitch!"

I decided to get in the shower, get fresh and go out and handle my business for the day.

CHAPTER 6

I had been on several runs today taking care of my business and picking money up. All my boys and workers wanted me to post up and kick it with them, but I didn't feel like it. It was now nearing midnight and Gryffyn still hadn't replied to my message, nor had she reached out. I can't even lie, the shit got me fucked up because I know I laid good pipe down, so she should've been tearing my line down to hear from me, damn near begging for some more of this.

Maybe she got busy or had to work or something. Shit, I don't even know if the girl has a job or not.

I had to shake thoughts of Gryffyn out of my head. I'm not no sucker ass nigga anyway.

Pulling up in front of my house, I parked and hopped out of my car, ready to retreat for the day. I was still a little tired from last night anyway. Once I made it inside and closed the door, I was instantly hit with flashbacks of Gryffyn being naked in those heels. I got hard just thinking about it. I kept on throughout my house and noticed we really did tear the crib up. The clothes I had on were strewn about. Stuff that was on the tables was now on the floor and so were the couch cushions. I proceeded to my bedroom and could still smell her. It's like her scent had been embedded in the walls. I took a second to think about the way she looked up at me during sex like I was the best thing since sliced bread.

"Damn, I want to be Christopher Columbus to that pussy! That shit is mine damnit, I was here first!"

Getting pissed off all over again, I decided to roll me a blunt and hop in the shower.

I sat down, began breaking my weed down and decided to turn on some music. Before I could tell Alexa what to play, my phone went off. I looked at it and noticed it was an unknown number. I put my now half-filled blunt down, picked my phone up with the quickness thinking that it was Gryffyn, and she somehow found my number and was calling. I cleared my throat and answered, "Yeah, who dis." It was the most unbothered voice I could muster up.

"Heyyyy nephew, you wouldn't happen to have something for me, would you? You can bring it to Irene's house."

"Man, Chris, get the fuck on, koo. I'm freeing up my line for something important. If you need something, hit P up!"

"Damn, nephew, who got your panties in a bunch today?"

I hung up the phone mad as hell!

Here I am thinking my baby done found me and it ain't nobody but Crackhead Chris trying to get high with his even bigger crackhead girlfriend Irene.

This is some bullshit, I thought while lighting my blunt.

What the fuck did this girl do to have me waiting by the phone? Last night I thought it was just the effects of the honey that had me tweaking, but that shit should've worn off by now. Whatever the case is, I'm not fucking with that shit no more. Last night that honey had me feeling like I was breaking Gryffyn's spine in half with my strokes, but clearly, she had the upper hand.

Look at me having one of those *hits blunt* moments. I've been stuck on this couch for almost thirty minutes thinking of all the ways Gryffyn and that honey had me fucked up.

I smashed the remainder of my wood into the ashtray and headed to the bathroom to get in the shower. I turned the hot water on and jumped right in. I was high as hell and the steam from the water made me feel so good inside. I reached down for my growing hard on and began stroking myself to thoughts of Gryffyn and the way she was riding my dick on a handstand. It had never been done before and thoughts of her wet, tight slit sent me into a frenzy. I rubbed and tugged on my meat until the nut fell from my muscle and I almost fell into the shower door. Maybe the honey was still in effect because I've been a horny ass beast all day. Every time I think of Gryffyn, I get hard and want to get one off.

"Man, where the fuck is shorty at!" I groaned.

I turned the water off, wrapped a towel around my tight muscular frame and walked into my bedroom. I reached over to my bedside refrigerator, grabbed my bottle of *Dussé* out, opened it and began drinking from it, straight from the bottle. The smoothness of the liquid goodness felt good going down. I needed something to take the edge off and put me to sleep. After a few swigs, the liquor set in and I was out like a light, with thoughts of Gryffyn floating around my head.

Two days later….

"Come in!"

I knew exactly who was at the door when I heard the three rapid knocks and the doorbell going off. Only one person did shit like that to purposely irritate me, and I had already been expecting him. We had some business to discuss as well as count up the profit from the week.

"What up, nigga?"

"What's up, bro," I greeted P.

I placed my gun, which was sitting on my lap, on top of the glass coffee table when I realized P was alone and resumed smoking my blunt. Even though P was my boy, I would never be caught off guard, after all, this is Chicago that we live in.

"Uh, is you cool nigga?" P asked and sat the duffle bag of what had better be nothing but money on the table in front of me, next to the money counter.

"Yeah, why you ask that?"

"My boy, you're hitting that wood hard as hell. Smoking that bitch like you're one of the fiends out there."

"Man, shut the fuck up. Ain't nobody doing all of that, here you go with the jokes and shit, man."

"Okay, okay dawg, chill out. What, or should I say who, got you all tight today?"

"Nobody, nigga, I'm good!"

P was now looking at me like I had two heads on my shoulders.

"Aight nigga let's count this shit up so I can get out of here then. I told shorty from the other night that we could chill tonight. Did you end up with any motion that night?" P asked while sparking up his own wood.

It was quiet in the house with the exception of the money machine as we passed our blunts in rotation.

This was common for us, P knew that if he started a rotation, then I would follow suit and we would get into some deep shit. That's why he was the only nigga that I called a brother. This was a hood nigga's version of therapy.

"So, what's up bro, you cool?" P asked again as he blew out a cloud of smoke and passed the blunt back to me.

"Yeah man, these bitches got me fucked up, my nigga." I dropped my head ashamed by the fact that this is really my life right now. Pressed about a female.

"Damn boy, it be like that sometimes, but you gotta shake that shit, dawg. Bitches come and go."

"Naw bro, this one was different, her pussy and even the way she looked at me was on a whole different type of time."

"Um, I don't even know what to say to that because you never speak on hoes like this. What the fuck makes her so different though? Pussy is pussy." P lit another blunt, inhaled and then blew the smoke out again.

"Here man, take this blunt, let's count this money and hit the strip club or something later. I can't have my brother out here looking pathetic like this."

"Bro, I'm fucked up, no cap. Earlier today I had me a drank, listening to some music, and this song by some sad ass bitch named Summer Walker was on. Her ass was saying some shit about drinking Patron and calling a nigga's phone. G, next thing I knew I was sliding down the wall, missing my lil stink on some nut shit. I was straight up under the female act," I chuckled reminiscing about my goofy ass meltdown earlier. "I fuck with shorty's music, though, lowkey."

I finally looked up and caught the confusion plastered all across P's face.

"Say something, nigga, don't just stare at me."

"You are officially pussy whipped, nigga, that's all I got for now. Trust me, I've been there a time or two- hundred before. I definitely got jokes for days though, but I won't laugh at my brother's pain right now. In the meantime, we're going to count up this bread, go see some naked bitches and get drunk."

"Shit, that sounds like a plan to me."

The next two hours consisted of counting, recounting and separating money. The mood did become a little lighter once I told my brother and best-friend what was going on with me. I looked down and noticed Vysion calling me, yet again.

"Man, Vysion been calling me every day! I know her ass don't want shit!" I grew annoyed.

"Nigga, this is a pattern between y'all. You should be used to it by now."

"Naw, G, it's different this time. I feel like that nigga on that one show that told his wife to chill and have some respect because he lost the love of his life. I'm focused on finding shorty right now, Vys can wait. She ain't going nowhere anyway." I silenced the call and resumed working.

Me and P finished up around 7pm. We sat around smoking and talking shit for another two hours before he dapped me up and went home to get ready for the strip club. We agreed on taking separate cars because we both liked pulling up to the spots with fresh car washes and the music beating loudly through the speakers. We loved the attention that women gave us when they saw two young, fine, getting money ass niggas hopping out of foreign whips.

P's goal was to leave the spot with a stripper or two, meanwhile, I was just trying to get my mind off of Gryffyn. I secretly hoped that I would run into her, which was the real reason I agreed to come out tonight. I don't even know if she goes to strip clubs or not, I just want to accidentally, on purpose bump into her, so I can figure out why the fuck she's playing with me.

I jumped out of my car first and P followed suit. We approached the security guards who already knew us and were on the payroll. They never really patted us down and knew we were going to take our straps everywhere we went, and we paid them well to turn a blind eye. We dapped them up and walked into the strip club, where as soon as we were visible, the dancers came from every direction wanting to be chosen for the night. I was uninterested so I nodded my head to the beat of The Great Future Hendrix' banger *"Freak Hoes,"* and walked over to one of the sections that P and I often occupied, leaving him with the girls.

I sat back, kicked my feet up and just like clockwork the waitress walked up and took my drink order.

"Just keep bottles of *Dussé* flowing tonight, sweetheart." I said without even acknowledging her. I just wanted to get drunk and vibe. I pulled my blunt out and began breaking it down.

"Uh, so that's it, Syxx? You aren't even going to speak to me?"

I was caught off guard by her saying my name with such disdain, so I looked up to see who the fuck this bitch was.

"Fuck you mean, is that it? Yeah, that's it! What's your problem shorty, you know me or something?"

"My problem is, you fucked me in the private room almost two months ago on some drunk shit, got me pregnant and blocked me when I tried to hit you up and tell you what was going on!"

"Oh, well are you still pregnant?" I asked even though I didn't really give a fuck.

"Hell naw! I went downtown and got an abortion since I couldn't get in touch with you and motherfuckers were acting too scared to give out your whereabouts!"

"Okay cool, then like I said, keep those bottles in rotation for me, love. Oh, and here's a tip." I reached into my pocket and pulled out a few blue faces, attempting to hand them to the bitter Betty before me.

"Fuck you!" She shouted and walked off.

"Let you tell it, I did." I shrugged and focused my attention back on rolling up.

I honestly had no recollection of fucking that girl. I don't doubt her story though. Thinking back on it, that's probably why Vysion had been calling so much. She probably got word about this shit too. Now I know I need to call her crazy ass back sooner than later, before she pops up at my front door thinking I had a baby on the way.

"Aye, why the fuck was the waitress crying, talking about they'll send us another one over?" P walked up with two of the dancers looking lost.

I shrugged my shoulders and passed him the blunt.

Every time we come to this spot our section gets bombarded by strippers looking for a come up, niggas looking for a plug or people just wanting to share the same space as us and look cool. Tonight, was no different, everybody was having a good time, except me. P was so gone off the liquor, he was letting the dancers pour packs of honey in his drinks. He knew he was hitting both dancers and was ensuring that he was going to handle them both. I'm sure he'll have a good story to tell tomorrow. All I could do was shake my head. I don't want no parts of that honey after the other night.

Tonight, was a complete bust for me. Even paying for multiple lap dances didn't help my mood. I turned down head and sex from the nastiest bitches in here, but I only wanted to feel one vagina. The one that belonged to Gryffyn Davis. That damn girl has me in a chokehold.

After about another hour of just sitting there looking slow I decided to leave. There was no point in me staying, I wasn't having no kind of fun. I can get drunk by myself in the crib.

"Aye, boy, I'm about to head out. You cool?"

"Damn, nigga, we just got here and you're leaving already? Get you one of these freaks and chill."

"Yeah, boo, come have some fun with us," One of the girls on P's lap motioned me near her.

"Naw, baby girl, maybe next time."

"Yo wtf, bro!" P was livid.

"Aight nigga, I'm out." I held my fist out to P for some dap, not caring about that nigga's attitude.

'Mmcht," P sucked his teeth and lightly slapped my hand down.

"Gon head with that, bruh, come relax." P was visibly frustrated.

"I'm gone, koo."

I turned around laughing at P's antics and walked out of the loud club. I can't lie, if I was in a better mood tonight would've been a movie. However, I'm just not feeling it.

I made it to my car and pushed the button allowing the engine to come to life. All I could do was shake my head at myself, because I am truly unrecognizable even to myself. I sparked up yet another blunt and began my journey home.

CHAPTER 7

One week later...

Syxx Tha OG: So, you can't even reach out and let a nigga know you're good? You on some good bullshit, G, that's crazy!

That was the fourth message in two days that I'd sent Gryffyn via her social media DM's. Her goofy ass hasn't replied to shit, and I know that nothing crazy has happened to her because I can see that she's been active on all of her social media, posting pictures and shit. She's really playing games with me like a nigga won't snatch her ass up!

I tried to give it some time and space but enough is enough. I need my bitch back! I don't even care if she has a nigga, I'll knock that nigga clean the fuck out! I'm not even sharing that pussy; it belongs to me!

Man, this bitch got me sounding and acting crazy. I can't worry about it though because it'll all work out in the end. I just have to get in touch with her ass.

Syxx The OG: G, you need to hit me back. We need to talk; I think I might've gotten you pregnant. I didn't pull out that night and we for damn sure didn't use no rubber.

I was desperate now, willing to say anything to get a response from her. This shit was becoming one big ass game. Me messaging Gryffyn, Vysion calling me non-stop, and ain't nobody getting what they want. Every time I saw Vysion's name across my screen, it pissed me off more and more because that's not who the fuck I want! This shit was throwing my energy all off!

I even had to smack the hell out of Crackhead Chris yesterday. I was out on the block posted up on my car with P, waiting on a couple of moves and this nigga walked up to me talking about, *"Nephew, you haven't been yourself lately. You look like you're stressed out behind either some ass or some money, which one is it, youngblood?"*

"Man, Chris, if you don't get your ass from around here with that shit." I was instantly agitated.

P laughed.

"Naw, neph, I'm for real, I know the look; Irene done had me in my feelings quite a few times back in our hay day."

"Alright Chris, what do you need, G?" I was ready for him to get away from me now.

Chris walked up to me as if he wanted to tell me something that he didn't want anyone else to hear, so I leaned in and the nigga had the nerve to whisper, loudly might I add, "If you need to get one off, I'll let you get Irene for a few hours, nephew. I'll need a lil incentive though." Chris then reached in for a hug.

Not only did a crackhead just try to hug me, but to offer me his crackhead girlfriend in exchange for some dope was beyond me! That was it, I saw red and slapped the shit out of Chris! His dope fiend ass took the blow like a man though, I must admit.

P was literally rolling on the ground, holding his stomach laughing.

"Damn, nephew, my bad! I was just trying to help. You look like you need some good lovin' in your life," Chris was now holding his jaw. "Let me get something from you though, nephew, damn!"

I ended up feeling bad about hitting Chris because I know his intentions were good and my anger was displaced. Chris had been a loyal client of mine for years. I apologized to him and gave him his drugs for free.

Chris didn't give a fuck one way or another, he took his freebie and ran off, in search of Irene, I'm sure.

I just needed Gryffyn to say something. Shit, even if she tells me that I gave her the worst dick she ever had and that it's fuck me, I still wanted to hear something from her fine ass.

My stomach started growling and that's when it hit me that I'd been doing more drinking and smoking than eating actual food. I hopped in the car and decided to go get some nachos from Western Tacos. I knew that I had been taking a chance at seeing Vysion because it's one of our go-to places to eat late night. It's now nearing 11 pm so Vysion's homebody ass should be in the house. I pulled into the drive- thru and ordered my food. It always takes a long time to get your order from here because there's always a line full of people. Tonight was no different, so I put my car in park and began rolling up so I could have an appetite and really eat. I sat in line for about ten minutes and then it was my turn at the window. I gave the cashier my money and glanced over to my right catching two thick ass bitches hopping out of what appears to be a brand-new Chevy Camaro. It's dark out so I can't really tell what the exact color is, but the two women with the fat asses were switching sides. The one on the driver's side was getting in the passenger seat and vice versa. I couldn't get a good look because of the time of night doubled with the five percent tint on my car, but I could have sworn that one of the women was Vysion. Before I could roll down my window to make sure, the cashier was handing me my food.

By the time I looked back over to where the girls were, they were pulling off. The license plate on the car did catch my attention however, because it was a Texas plate that read "DAT 1."

I sat back in my seat knowing damn well I didn't just see Vysion, I thought.

"Nah," I shook my head and pulled off.

Vysion is boring and don't be outside like that if it's not me bringing her out.

I sparked my weed back up and headed home tweaking on the fact that I really be addressing Vysion like we are or have ever been in a relationship.

"Bitches are going to be the death of me, man."

There weren't many cars out tonight, I assume because it's a Sunday night, so it took me no time to get home, but the images of the two females at the restaurant had plagued my brain, probably making the drive a much shorter one. I can confidently say that I know that bubble of an ass that sits on Vysion's back is recognizable from anywhere. The only thing that has me unsure, however, is the fact that she doesn't hang around very many people, so the other mystery girl is a question mark to me. Especially someone with Texas license plates. I shook it off and headed into the house. I walked in, kicked off my sneakers and plopped down on the couch with my food. I'd already had a half liter of Hennessy on the glass table from previous drinking binges, so I turned on some sports highlights, ate my food, and poured myself some shots.

It was around 1:00 a.m. when my buzzing phone woke me up from a nap that I hadn't known I was taking. It took a few seconds for me to realize that I had fallen asleep on the couch. I grabbed my phone from beside me and glanced at the name on the screen. P was calling and although I hadn't spoken to him since that night at the club, I knew that he had to be calling at this hour for something important. I answered the call and instantly knew that P was outside somewhere because of the loud music and people talking in the background.

"Yo," I answered clearing my throat to get the grogginess out.

"Aye, nigga, you sleep?"

"Yeah, I guess I nodded off but what's good, koo?"

"Aye bro, your girl up here at the after-hours spot in the parking lot acting up."

"Who, Gryffyn?" I sat straight up ready for P to tell me he had spotted my baby somewhere. I was ready to pull up and snatch her up by her wig, shit her hot girl summer was ending tonight.

"Nigga, who? I never got a chance to meet the shorty you've been fucked up about, so I don't know how she looks. I'm talking about Vys. She's up here with some fine ass chocolate bitch. They up here talking to niggas and shaking ass and shit. Shorty up here on some other type of time too, bro. I see them mixing honey packs in their liquor and taking shots. This ain't even Vysion's character that I know of. I damn near wanna go get at ol' girl though, because she's fine and thick as fuck. Vys got on some little ass shorts too, what you want me to do, bro?"

"Aye, bro, drop me your dot. I'm on my way."

I jumped up, went into the bathroom to brush my teeth, grabbed my keys and headed out to see what exactly was going on. True enough Vysion ain't my bitch and I had been ignoring her for weeks, but she's not about to be out here wilding the fuck out either. Secondly, her ass doesn't ever be out this late and to top it off, she's outside being a hoe. This is truly weird ass behavior coming from her and I'm not used to her acting out of body, and in public too? I'm going to check her ass.

It took me seven minutes to arrive at the after-hours spot where they were. I'm pretty ashamed of myself for being in the house sleep like an unc, when it was bussing out here, actually. The parking lot was jam packed and summertime Chi was in full effect. I located P and a few niggas from around the way. I parked my car alongside P's, got out and dapped the guys up. They had blunts and bottles in full rotation. As soon as P saw me looking around for Vysion, he handed me one of the bottles and a blunt, insisting that I pour up.

"You gon need this, bro. Just chill though, but if you move, we all move."

"Man bro, I ain't even on that. I just want to see what the fuck has gotten into Vysion," I inhaled hard and blew the smoke out, almost choking.

"See bro, here you go hitting the Za like a fiend again," P joked, "These bitches are really doing a number on you man."

"Nigga, shut the," I paused when I glanced over P's shoulder.

My eyes had to have been playing tricks on me because I spotted Vysion, but she was sitting on top of the Camaro I had seen earlier today at the restaurant. My stomach dropped at the sight of who she was with.

"Gryffyn," I mumbled.

"What, nigga? Why are you whispering? You cool, nigga?"

"Bro, the thick bitch over there with Vysion is Gryffyn. The bitch I've been searching high and low for."

P shook his head at the new revelation and reached into his car to pulled out another blunt from his car stash. He lit it, took a long pull and blew it out presenting a thick cloud of smoke.

"Damn, brodie," he shook his head again, "You think they're fucking or some shit?"

"Man, I don't know but I'm definitely about to find out."

"You got your strap on you right?" Concern was etched on P's face.

"Always, bro, I'll be right back."

Karma

CHAPTER 8

I stalked across the parking lot, with a thousand thoughts running through my head. There was literally no valid explanation as to why these two were kicking it. Then a part of me wanted to slap the shit out of Gryffyn for ghosting me, but the other part was just glad to see her fine ass in person. Either way, both of these bitches were going to have to tell me something before I aired this whole parking lot out.

The closer I got to them, the more agitated I became because both of my bitches were out here embarrassing me by entertaining these goofy ass niggas. Niggas that don't even know how fast they could lose their lives behind fucking with anything, or anyone attached to my name. I continued my trek, blunt in hand, not knowing what I was about to get into until finally I approached the crowd of people Vysion and Gryffyn were standing with. Neither one of them noticed me because they were too busy shaking ass. I flicked the remainder of my blunt away once I finished it.

"Excuse me, big dawg," I said to several onlookers as I made my way through the slew of people.

A few people recognized me and dapped me up. They must've caught on to the look in my eyes that meant business because once I shook up with them, they all dispersed and got out of dodge, which was probably the safest decision.

Gryffyn and Vysion were dancing on one another, clearly enjoying life, meanwhile Gryffyn has had me going bat shit crazy ever since she fucked me and forgot me. I walked up snatching Vysion off of Gryffyn.

"Aye, what the fuck?" A startled Vysion snatched away from me.

Both women looked as if they were ready to fuck me up until they recognized who I was.

"Uh, Syxx what are you doing out here and why are you putting your hands on me?" Vysion asked, shock still etched across her face.

"Naw, motherfucker. What are you doing out here, and with her?" I pointed to a quiet Gryffyn.

"And how do you even know her?"

"I'll get to you in a second!"

Gryffyn leaned against the car and sipped from her cup, with a smirk on her face.

"First of all, Syxx, stop talking to me like you're my damn daddy! I ain't never had one of those a day in life! Secondly, I've called you multiple times and you couldn't answer but now you wanna run up on me because you see me outside, right? Nigga you got me fucked up!"

"Naw, I saw you over here with my bitch being a hoe, so I came to get both of you in line. But you know what, you ain't even the reason I'm over here for real, move."

"You're bitch?" Vysion scoffed.

Honestly, Vysion wasn't my main concern, so I really didn't give a fuck about what she was talking about at the moment. I can get at her anytime.

I slid past Vysion and approached my baby. Her facial expression was stoic so I couldn't get a good read on her. She was now sitting on top of the trunk of the Camaro, cup still in hand.

"What's up, Syxx? You want some? It has one of those *honey pack's* that you like in it?" Gryffyn stuck her hand out in an attempt to hand me her cup.

"What's up? Stop playing in my face shorty. Why haven't I heard from you? I thought we were cool and had fun? Why did you disappear on a nigga? And naw I don't want none of that shit." I lightly smacked her hand away from me.

I had so many things in my head that I planned on saying to Gryffyn's ass when I finally caught up to her and now, I couldn't think of even one of them when it's necessary. All I could do is throw twenty-one questions at her ass. I can't front seeing her face and hearing her voice ignited something in me that I can't explain.

"Aw, Syxx, baby, you sound like you missed me," she smiled and slid off the car walking over to me. Vysion had now rejoined us as well.

"You think I'm a game or that this is a joke? Bitch, I ain't no damn punchline!" I fumed.

Gryffyn's tone was laced with sarcasm, and it was fucking with me. I was trying to be cool, but I felt my anger rising. That's when it hit me in the chest like a punch from Mayweather. The Texas license plates, Gryffyn just randomly hitting me in my DM, and her coincidently guessing my favorite breakfast foods was all a set up.

"Wait, hold the fuck up! You two bitches plotted on me?" I laughed at the irony but there really wasn't shit funny because I wanted to slap the hell out of both of them.

"Aye, koo, let's get out of here. Fuck these hoes." P appeared through the crowd of spectators who were tuned in to the show before them.

"Naw, nigga, I want them to answer the question! I wanna know what the fuck is going on!"

Vysion and Gryffyn both looked as though they were thoroughly enjoying this moment.

"Well Syxx, since we're all here now fuck it, I'll fill you in, babe. When my cousin Vysion told me all about you and how you mistreat and mishandle women I knew you needed to be humbled. I told Vysion that I would get you in line and for her to just follow my lead. You don't get to play with a beautiful and loyal woman the way you do and not have any consequences behind it. My cousin fucking loves you, nigga. So, I decided to treat you the way you treat women. Fuck you really good and then dismiss your trifling ass! I just took you on a test drive, daddy, but I was always going to leave you on the lot. It's Karma and niggas are easy, period."

Before I could even react to the gut-wrenching, ego shattering blow that Gryffyn delivered, Vysion grabbed Gryffyn's cup and took a sip from it.

"Whew!" Vysion grimaced. "That honey and Henny combo hits every time. How does it feel, Syxx?"

"How does what feel, Vysion?" I rolled my eyes wondering why she was even still talking to me right now.

I was still processing everything that Gryffyn hit me with, so Vysion's random question irritated me. Especially when I was already in the mood to knock her head off. P knew it was about to get bad, so he sparked up and handed me the blunt to smoke. I inhaled heavily and blew it back out. The high kicked in immediately and suddenly, I wasn't boiling so much internally. I hit it again, "Say what the fuck you gotta say, Vysion." I exhaled and choked a little on the smoke.

It was Gryffyn's turn to take the cup back and take a sip, with yet another smirk on her face as Vysion spoke.

"How does it feel to have that cherry popped, my love?"

I slapped the cup out of Gryffyn's hand. She held her hands up as if to surrender.

"You got it, baby."

Gryffyn took a step back, hands still up and laughing.

"Cherry? Vysion, what the fuck are you talking about?" I got in her face, and I felt P grab my shoulder. "Man, get off me bro," I said jerking away from P's grasp. I'm a grown ass man, don't ever say no shit like that to me again," I seethed and backed away.

"Nigga don't get your hoe ass back in my cousin's face," Gryffyn menacingly stated.

"Or what? Y'all two bitches got me fucked up and I should beat both of y'all's asses for playing with me. What did you think was going to happen? Did y'all think that this goofy ass plan was going to make me a better man and decide that all women are Black Queens and become some sucker ass nigga? Fuck both of you hoes, I'll have a new line up of bitches tomorrow!" I laughed in their dumb ass faces and turned to walk off.

"I bet they can't give you the best of both worlds like she can. The joke is on you."

Gryffyn and Vysion laughed as if someone had told them a joke.

"Right, because baby you'll never get a tighter pussy than mine and that's why your ass is obsessed with me now."

They slapped hands, laughter continuing.

I kept walking, "Y'all hoes are dumb!"

"Yo, you good bro?" P asked as we walked back to our cars.

"Yeah, koo, I'm good. I don't know what they thought was supposed to happen. I fuck hoes on a regular basis, they are not stopping shit. Shorty did have some good ass pussy though; I will miss that. As for Vysion, while she's over there capping, she'll be ready to suck my dick tonight if I call her phone and tell her to."

"Facts, bro," P laughed and re-lit the blunt he handed me back when I was going at it with dumb and dumber.

"Vysion was saying some weird shit though, koo. Did you peep it?"

"I wasn't paying any attention to Vysion, because unlike Gryffyn, Vysion is in love with my ass so all that rah-rah shit she be talking is all bullshit."

"Yeah, I feel you bro," P nodded as we both unlocked our car doors to get in.

The crowd was dispersing little by little, which gave me an easier view of the parking lot. I saw Gryffyn and Vysion still over there drinking and kicking it. I shook my head again and was beyond ready to get away from here.

Me and P went in for a hug and handshake.

P began to chuckle.

"What are you laughing at, nigga?"

"Nigga, they were on your ass, boy!" P laughed loudly this time.

"That damn girl gon tell you got your cherry popped, like what the fuck, G?"

"Motherfucka's only say that when it's a first time for some shit, nigga you been getting pussy, so what was new?"

P had a whole lot to say right when I'm high as hell and ready to leave. He was actually cracking himself up, too.

Now that he mentioned it, what the hell was Vysion talking about? A cherry, wait hold on. I closed my car door, in the middle of P's laugh fest, turned on the heels of my Jay's, and headed back in the direction of Vysion and Gryffyn. P was on my heels looking confused.

Neither girl was expecting me to come back, so when I did, the conversation they were having were ceased. They both saw me and turned towards me.

"What do you want, Syxx" Vysion popped off first.

"Why was you talking about a cherry being popped?"

Gryffyn laughed and walked to the Camaro.

"I knew you were slow, nigga. You don't get it yet, do you?" Vysion chimed.

"Get what, girl, damn! Just say the shit so I can go."

"You did get your cherry popped, nigga."

"You didn't notice how tight this pussy hole is, nigga? It is new," Gryffyn yelled from the passenger seat. "Come on, Vysion. Leave his ass right there, lost as ever."

"I don't even care anymore; fuck it, I'm gone. Ya'll playing and I'm too high to play this guessing game. Fuck y'all!"

I was agitated, high and just ready to get away from these damn girls so I turned to leave again.

"Well, you fucked Gryff's brand new pussy, because she ditched the dick, as me and her call it."

"Ditched what?" I turned back around and asked, wondering if I'd heard her correctly.

"My cousin used to have a penis, dummy!"

"You're the first one in the city to try it out, you like it?" Vysion jokingly asked.

"Yo, Vysion, quit fucking playing with me," I snapped.

"I guess it's safe to say you were *doing the bending*."

Vysion turned, and headed to the waiting car, as P and all of the remaining people that were outside looked at me for some sort of reaction. All I felt at that moment was the heat of the blood that was boiling in my veins. I saw red instantly.

I know this bitch didn't stand here and tell me that I was fucking, sucking and trying to love on somebody that was born just like?

"Man, ain't no way," I stated quietly to myself and began walking in the direction of where Vysion was about to get inside of the car. The length of my legs allowed me ability to make it to them in four strides. I pulled my gun from the lining of my pants, and before either of them could fully ask what was going on, I let off two shots into the skulls of Vysion and Gryffyn, killing them instantly. Before anybody could say anything to me or me having to sit and think about what just went down, I let off a third shot. It was into my own skull. I can't go out bad like that.

The End.

OTHER BOOKS BY THE AUTHOR.

Faulty Fallon

Trick-or-Treat: A Halloween Sexcapade

https://www.amazon.com/author/a.monique

Don't forget to leave a review!

Made in the USA
Columbia, SC
24 November 2024